JANETTA OTTER-BARRY BOOKS

Aesop's Fables copyright © Frances Lincoln Limited 2011
Text copyright © Beverley Naidoo 2011
Illustrations copyright © Piet Grobler 2011

First published in Great Britain and in the USA in 2011 by
Frances Lincoln Children's Books, 4 Torriano Mews,
Toriano Avenue, London NW5 2RZ
www.franceslincoln.com

A catalogue record of this book is available from the British Library.

ISBN 978-1-84780-007-7

Illustrated with pencil and watercolours

Printed in Dongguan, Guangdong, China by Toppan Leefung in December 2010

1 3 5 7 9 8 6 4 2

AESOP'S FABLES

Beverley Naidoo

Piet Grobler

F

FRANCES LINCOLN
CHILDREN'S BOOKS

CONTENTS

Dear Reader

I was hooked by Aesop's fables when I was a child. I knew a lot of the animals in his tales because I grew up in South Africa. We lived down the road from the city zoo but it was more exciting to spot lions, snakes and eagles out in the bush. We had cunning jackals rather than Aesop's "foxes" and grumpy warthogs instead of "boars", but really they were much the same animals. Aesop's fables often sent a shiver through me and I loved them!

Who was Aesop? The grown-ups – and my books – said that he was a wise slave who had lived over two and a half thousand years ago in Greece. So I thought of him as Greek. I didn't pick up other clues, such as…

Why does Aesop have African animals in so many of his fables?

Most of his fables have a moral and African folk tales often show us the meaning of a proverb.

Aesop's fables aren't like fairy tales from Europe with "happy ever after" endings. They are much more like traditional African stories. Life is tough… and things can end badly for anyone who doesn't watch out or use their wits!

Nowadays I think that Aesop was African. He was probably captured somewhere in North Africa and forced to go to Greece. His name sounds like the old Greek word for a black African: "Ethiop". Some say that he was so wise and witty that his master freed him and that he became an adviser to the king. We don't really know. But of one thing we are sure. While his masters are long forgotten, Aesop's name and fables live on. People still hear them, love them, and want to tell them again. So, my turn now… and your turn next!

Beverley Naidoo

The Old Lion

An old lion was too weak to go out and catch his own food. Once upon a time, his wives hunted for the family while he guarded their home. But now they had died and all their cubs had grown up and gone their own ways. All alone, he found a cave where he lay down, pretending to be very ill.

"Oooohhhh!" he moaned. In between each moan, he listened for sounds outside, but heard nothing.

"Aaaaagghhh!" he groaned, this time a little louder.

A herd of zebras, grazing in the long grass, pricked up their ears and began to shift away. However there was one young zebra who trotted over to the cave. She was curious to see what was going on.

Well, as soon as she put her head around the rock to peer into the darkness, the old lion pulled her inside and that was the end of her. After that, whenever he was hungry, the old lion repeated his trick. It worked every time.

One day, however, a passing jackal heard the strange "Oooohhh!" and "Aaaaagghhh!". Quietly, she slunk towards the cave but wisely stopped a few feet away from the entrance.

"Is anybody there?" Jackal called.

"Aagghh, have pity! I'm very sick!" whined Old Lion. "Come inside and help me, please!"

"My friend," replied Jackal, "I would have helped you. But I see that there are many footprints pointing into your cave – and none that come out! So, excuse me, I shall just carry on my way."

~ Not everyone is fooled by an old trick. ~

THE Eagle and the Tortoise

Tortoise was fed up with his life. He was bored with being a tortoise.

"I'm tired of crawling on the ground all the time," he grumbled to Eagle, who had stopped to rest above him on the branch of a camel-thorn tree. "I want to soar through the air like you!"

"You're not built for flying," warned Eagle.

"I've watched how you birds do it," said Tortoise. "I can wave my flippers in the air. Just get me up there and I'll show you. If you do that for me, I'll bring you buried treasure."

Treasure! That did it. Grasping the tortoise with his sharp talons, Eagle carried him up into the sky. He flew higher and higher.

Aaaiiieee! Far below, the waterhole became a tiny puddle and a herd of elephants turned into ants! Tortoise didn't know whether to keep his eyes open or shut.

"Now then, let's see you fly!" cried Eagle and he loosened his grip. But the moment Tortoise was by himself, he fell like a stone, and when he struck the ground he was smashed into a thousand little pieces.

~ Just wishing for something doesn't make it happen. ~

The Dog, the Cock and the Jackal

A dog and a cock who lived on the same farm had become great friends. Every evening, the farmer locked all his hens and the cock inside a large wire coop to keep them safe from the wild animals on the nearby mountain. Jackals were always looking for a chance to slink through the shadows of the orange grove so that they could burrow their way into the hen run. But first they had to get past the dog that guarded the farmhouse and the coop.

One night, when the dog had been busy chasing something else, a jackal managed to slip through and escape with a hen. Early the next morning, the farmer saw the scattered feathers and found the hole that the jackal had scraped under the wire.

"You useless brak! What's wrong with you?" he blasted the poor dog. "Just wait. When I find a better guard, you can go begging for your food somewhere else!"

The cock heard the farmer's threat and felt sorry for his friend. After the farmer stormed away, the cock crowed softly to the dog.

"Don't worry, man," he tried to comfort him. "The two of us can go away and look for another farm. I've always wanted to go places. See things. What do you say?"

The dog agreed. His future didn't look too bright here any more. So when the farmer went into the kitchen for his coffee, the two friends sneaked away. They kept just off the road, not wanting to get lost deep in the bush. The cock found bits of grain and an old mealie cob to peck, while the dog picked up a few scraps here and there. There were new sights to see and they were happy wandering onwards. They wanted to get far away from the angry farmer before looking for a new farm.

At the end of the day, as the sun dipped towards the far end of the valley and the purple blanket of night descended, they found a good place to rest. It was a fat baobab tree with a hole inside big enough for the dog.

"Ho ho!" sang the cock. "I'll roost on top and you can curl up safely inside. No worries!"

Soon they were both fast asleep.

As usual, the cock woke at the break of day and began to crow.

But, oh my! As his eyes got used to the early morning shadows, he saw a jackal approaching. It was hard to keep his crowing steady.

"Sjoe! But you have a wonderful voice!" praised the jackal. "I should like to know someone who sings so beautifully."

The cock stopped crowing and nodded. "No problem, why don't you wake up my doorman who sleeps at the foot of my tree," he suggested. "He'll open the door and let you in."

So the jackal tapped on the trunk of the tree.

Immediately the dog woke up, rushed out and tore the jackal to pieces.

~ A friend in need is a friend indeed. ~

brak – a mongrel dog (Afrikaans)
mealie – corn
Sjoe! – Amazing!

The Mosquito and the Lion

It was a very hot afternoon and Lion, King of the Bushveld, had finished eating a large meal. With a deep purr he stretched himself out to sleep under the shade of a bushy sweet-thorn tree. This was the life!

However, a tiny mosquito began buzzing around his head. When Lion opened one eye and swiped at it with his great paw, the little creature simply danced aside.

"What a fine, strong king you are!" Mosquito jeered. "Ha! Show me your claws and teeth! You can't even catch me!"

Lion was furious and tried harder to strike Mosquito. Yet every time he attempted to whack the tiny beast, it zigzagged past him.

"See, I'm stronger than you," Mosquito boasted. "Watch me!"

With that, he dived down and bit Lion on his nose. Letting out a mighty roar, Lion thrust out his claws further. But instead of catching the little fellow, he scratched the skin from his own nose. As he bled, the stinging was much worse than Mosquito's bite.

Mosquito shrieked with laughter. "What did I tell you? Wait until everyone hears about this!"

However, the little fellow did not get very far. Hurrying to boast of his victory, he flew into a spider's web and the spider stretched out to swallow him.

"Eishh, but I'm stupid!" cried Mosquito with his last breath. "I conquered the King himself but I am defeated by a mere spider."

~ Pride comes before a fall. ~

Eishh! – a bit like 'Oh dear!'

The Rinkhals and the Snake-Eagle

A snake-eagle was hovering high above a hill when his old yellow eyes spied a young rinkhals slither on to a rock to sun itself. In less than a second, the snake-eagle swooped down and seized the spitting cobra in its powerful claws. With his razor-sharp beak, the eagle tried to tear open the back of the snake's neck. But the rinkhals coiled and lashed out fiercely, striving to spit its poison into the eagle's black breast. It was a life or death struggle up in the air.

As the young rinkhals kept trying to strike, the old snake-eagle began to regret his action and wanted to let go of its prey. But the two of them were now interlocked. Perhaps they would both hurtle onto the rocks below and be smashed together.

Now, a young man was watching their struggle from below. He was on a long journey and had sat down to rest and drink. He placed his

gourd on the rock where the rinkhals had been going to sunbathe.

"If that snake-eagle hadn't snatched the snake, it might have killed me!" thought the young man. He wanted to help the eagle and pulled out his sling. He waited for the fighting pair to come lower. Then, using the smoothest of pebbles, he took aim.

The blow struck the rinkhals right between its eyes. Blinded for a moment, it gave up fighting. The exhausted eagle let it go and the rinkhals fell to the earth. Sjoe, it was still alive! As the young man turned to pick up his stick to beat it, the snake spat its poison into the man's water gourd before slithering away. By the time the young man looked up, the rinkhals was gone.

"Well, at least I saved that old snake-eagle," said the young man and picked up his gourd to drink his water. But as he lifted his hand, the great bird flew at him, almost knocking him over and spilling the poisoned water on the ground.

"Ha! Don't you know that I saved your life?" the young man called out indignantly as the snake-eagle flew away. He did not know that the old snake-eagle had saved his life as well.

~ One good turn deserves another. ~

rinkhals – a ring-necked spitting cobra

The Jackal and the Klipspringer

Jackal was climbing a mountain when he lost his footing on a loose rock and tumbled into a narrow kloof. Luckily a rocky platform stopped him from plunging all the way down the crevice, but there was no way that he could climb out. At least a little stream of water trickling through the kloof gave him something to drink.

By and by he heard a squeaky whistle. Was that a klipspringer up there? Jackal began to howl a little tune, loud enough to be heard and trying to sound happy. The klipspringer stretched his head over the edge of the rock above.

"What are you doing there?" asked Klipspringer.

"Aiee! Just enjoying the mountain water," laughed Jackal. "It's delicious, straight from the spring! Why don't you come and try it?"

Without stopping to think, Klipspringer leaped down on to the platform in the kloof and began to drink.

"You're right," said Klipspringer after he had finished drinking. "It's the best water I've tasted in a long time. I'd better be on my way."

But when Klipspringer looked up, he couldn't see a single foothold onto which he could leap. His heart jumped inside him, but he tried to hide his sudden fear.

"How do we get out?" he asked.

"That's not difficult if we work as a team," advised Jackal. "You stand on your back legs and press your forelegs up against the rock so that your horns are high in the air. I'll climb up your back and jump from your horns to the top. Then I can lean over and help pull you out."

Well, Klipspringer did as he was told. Jackal nimbly scampered up his companion and then jumped to safety with a yelp of delight.

"Now the water is all yours!" he called down to Klipspringer. He grinned, ready to sprint away.

"What about me?" Klipspringer squealed. "You promised to pull me out of here!"

"If you had as many brains in your head as bristles on your face," taunted Jackal, "you would never have jumped in without first thinking about how to get out."

With that, Jackal continued on his way, leaving poor Klipspringer to his fate.

~ Look before you leap. ~

Kloof – a gorge (Afrikaans)
Klipspringer – a 'rock jumper', a little antelope (Afrikaans)

The Lion and the Warthog

One blistering hot day in the middle of summer, Lion and Warthog had the same idea. Get down to the waterhole and drink! They arrived at the same time and at the very same spot.

"I go first!" growled Lion.

"Hayi khona! Oh no you don't!" retorted Warthog.

Lion roared, striking Warthog with his claws. But the small fellow jerked backwards, then charged with his tusks. Together they grappled, this way and that. It looked as if they would tear each other to death until, panting, each stopped to take breath.

The air was heavy. Glancing up at the tall trees around the waterhole, each saw a line of vultures quietly waiting. Eh!

"It's better to be friends," grumbled Lion.

"Yebo, my friend," agreed Warthog. "Who wants to fight and become food for vultures?"

~ It's safer to be friends than enemies. ~

Hayi khona – no way, Yebo – yes (isiZulu)

The Donkey, the Jackal and the Lion

Another day and still no rain! For months there had been no clouds in the sky while the sun beat down on the land below. Things were so bad that a jackal and a donkey agreed to look for food together. In the late afternoon, when the sun blushed and turned the brown earth blood-red, the pair would slink through the dry bush to the waterhole. Day by day, as the water shrank, fewer animals came to drink. Some animals even decided to trek across the mountains, hoping that the rains had come to the next valley.

Sometimes Donkey would spot the body of an animal lying stock-still in the grass ahead. He would bray and Jackal would creep up and set upon the poor creature, whether it was alive or dead. Then Jackal would have a feast. In return, he would spy little plants here and there that Donkey could enjoy.

But, in the end, they decided that they too would have to try their luck trekking over the mountain. Jackal sprinted ahead, sniffing out the route that the other animals had taken. Every now and again he turned and yapped so that Donkey would know where to follow. Climbing higher along a rocky path, he came to a fork. Left or right?

On the right were steep rocks. Going left looked easier, with a small bridge made of wooden branches. However, he was suddenly reminded of a hunter's trap! He patted the bridge with his front paw and, sure enough, it trembled.

He was about to run back and warn Donkey when he sensed that he was not alone. A lion with large hungry eyes was blocking his way.

"Good day, my friend," said Jackal quickly. "Times are bad, hey? You look so thin!"

The lion said nothing. He flicked his tongue across his teeth.

"Let's make a plan, my friend," Jackal persisted. "You know, you and I would make a fantastic team."

The lion's stomach rumbled.

"Look, man," Jackal was getting a little nervous now. "I can get you the best meal that you've had in a long time! You won't have to do a thing. Just hide here where no one can see you." Jackal pointed to a large rock near the false bridge. "Watch me! I'll show you what I mean."

Jackal's heart skipped a beat as the lion lumbered towards him, fixing Jackal with those famished eyes. But at the last moment, the lion slouched past him and lay down behind the rock. Jackal now waited on the other side of the rock, gazing back the way he had come. As soon as he saw Donkey's ears appear, he called out.

"I've been waiting for you, my friend."

"Thank you," panted Donkey, who was sweating. "I couldn't have made it this far without you."

"Don't worry," said Jackal. "I've checked the way ahead. It's over the bridge. You can go first!" He lowered his eyes so that Donkey wouldn't see into them.

Donkey trotted past him and, as he stepped on to the bridge, the wooden branches gave way. With a pitiful bray, he tumbled down into the pit below.

"You can come out now," sang Jackal. "Your dinner is ready!"

The lion prowled out from his hiding place. He took one glance at the helpless donkey in the pit and then brought his enormous paw crashing down on the jackal. He ate Jackal first and, for his second course, he feasted on Donkey.

~ If you betray a friend, don't be surprised
when someone betrays you. ~

The Cat and the Mice

It was the middle of winter, and a hungry cat was seeking shelter and food when she came across an old farmhouse. There was no one around, and the thatch on the roof looked as mangy and shabby as her fur. If the place was deserted, she could at least try her luck inside. So she slunk to the door and peered between the broken planks.

Yislaaik!!! There were mice everywhere! They were running back and forth, all over the floor, from one end to the other.

"Just the place for me," the cat meowed to herself and stepped inside. Beside the door was a pile of old sacks that kept her hidden. She caught one mouse, then another, and another. How simple! What a treat!

But at last, the mice realised the danger.

"Hide! Hide!" they squealed. Some scurried to find a hole in the wall. Others scuttled upwards to hide in the thatch. Soon there was not a mouse to be seen.

"I need to make a plan," said the cat, and sat down to think. Her olive-green eyes wandered around the room until they fixed on a wooden peg sticking out of the wall. Aha! The farmer used to hang his coat on that peg. She could hang herself from the peg and pretend to be dead. Then the mice would relax and come out to play again.

Up leaped the cat, very nimbly now that she had warmed up after a few tasty morsels. Swinging her feet over the peg, she hung upside down and waited. Soon the mice would come scampering back, silly mamparas. But all was quiet. Nothing happened. Finally, from the corner of her eye she glimpsed a very small mouse peeping out from a hole.

"Madam!" he squeaked.

The cat tried not to breathe. It's not easy to pretend that you are an old fur coat.

"You are very clever to hang there like a bag of flour!" piped the little mouse.

A bag of flour! What a cheek, thought the cat! Just wait till she snapped up that little laaitie! It was an effort for her to stay still.

"You hang there as long as you like, Madam," continued the mouse. "But you won't catch us coming near you again!"

"Meeeooowwww!" The cat swung herself off the peg and landed in front of the hole in the wall.

A cluster of tiny eyes shivered in front of her but out of reach. Were they scared. . . or were they laughing at her? It was impossible to tell. To be honest, she felt a bit of a mampara herself. But she wouldn't let them see! So, lifting her nose, she padded out of the door into the cold.

~ Once bitten, twice shy. ~

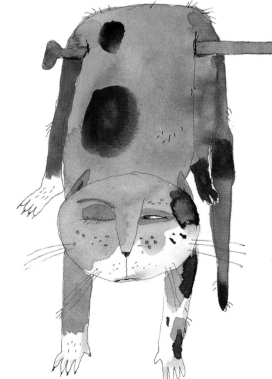

Laaitie – youngster (South African slang)
Mampara – fool (South African slang)

The Monkey and the Fishermen

A monkey sat high in a tree, watching a band of fishermen cast their nets into a river. The men stood silently for a while and then pulled in their nets filled with fish.

"Easy, man!" Monkey said to himself. "I can do that!"

So he waited until the fishermen were tired. They left their nets on the bank and came to rest in the shade of the trees. Swiftly Monkey skipped down from his look-out branch and hurried towards the nets.

Sure that he could copy the fishermen, he quickly lifted a net and slung it towards the water. But in doing this, he got himself caught up in the ropes and toppled over the bank into the river.

"Why did I go fishing without knowing how to fish?" Monkey cried to himself in his last moments, before drowning.

~ Don't meddle in something that you don't understand. ~

The Farmer and his Children

An old farmer knew that he would soon die, and he was worried that his children would not take proper care of the land he had loved. So he called them to his side.

"My children," he whispered, "I am about to die. But I want you to know that hidden among my fruit trees is something of great value. Dig well and you will find it."

The children imagined that their father had buried a treasure. So, as soon as he was dead and placed to rest in the little graveyard on the farm, they began to dig. There had been little rain and the red earth was hard, but they kept at it, turning the soil over and over until not a bit was left unturned.

They found nothing. But because the soil was dug so well, the fruit trees bore wonderful fruit for many years to come.

~ Work is the real treasure. ~

The Farmer and the Jackal

A farmer was fed up with a jackal that prowled down from the mountain at night and, one by one, silently stole his hens. So he stayed awake all night, waiting and waiting, feeling more and more angry. Early in the morning, with just the first hint of light, he saw a shadowy figure slip past him, heading for the hen run.

The farmer followed quietly and watched where the jackal dug a hole under the fence. He was determined to catch it, even if it meant losing one more hen. So he let the creature squeeze through the hole and scamper into the run, and then he blocked the exit with a trap. It wasn't long before the jackal returned, a hen hanging between her jaws. Scrabbling through the hole, she realised too late that she had been caught. Eishh! She dropped the dead bird and howled to send a message to her young ones on the mountain.

Instead of killing the jackal right away, the farmer wanted her to suffer. So he soaked a rope in paraffin and tied it to the jackal's tail. Then, setting the rope alight, he let her go. Ha! The creature would soon be on fire and that would teach her a lesson!

But the jackal ran straight through the farmer's field with his golden mealies ready for harvest. Before he could do anything, the ripe cobs caught fire; one stalk, then the next, and the next.

The unforgiving farmer never found out what happened to the jackal, whether she managed to put out the fire on her tail, or not. However, he was sure of one thing. He lost his whole crop of mealies… and that cost him a great deal more than the hens he had lost to the jackal and her family.

~ *Revenge is a two-edged sword.* ~

The Kudu at the Waterhole

It was another hot afternoon, and a thirsty kudu came down to the waterhole to drink. Leaning over the water, he caught sight of his reflection.

"What fabulous horns!" Kudu told himself. "My legs are thin as sticks and look feeble and ordinary. But my curling horns are really something!"

He was so busy admiring himself that he failed to see Lion creeping down to the waterhole. As Lion pounced, Kudu leaped away, his legs carrying him as fast as they could. Lion gave chase. As long as Kudu was running through the grass on the open veld, his strong legs kept him ahead of Lion. But suddenly he was faced with a thicket of bushes and when he tried to dash his way through them, his great horns became entangled in branches.

Seconds later, he felt Lion's teeth and claws rip into him.

In his last moments, Kudu said to himself, "What a fool I am! The legs that I despised could have saved me but the horns that I admired have led to my death."

~ What you take for granted may be much more valuable than you think. ~

Kudu – a large grey antelope (from iqudu in isiXhosa)
Veld – grassland (Afrikaans)

The Tamboti and the Reeds

A tall tamboti tree grew on the banks of a river. Tamboti's wood was mighty strong, so farmers prized it when building homes for their families and shelters for their animals. However, the tree's milky sap was also poisonous. There were stories of people who had touched it, rubbed their eyes and gone blind. Tamboti was very proud of having kept so many sharp axes away.

But one night, in a fierce and terrible storm, it was uprooted by a gale. It was thrown across the water and came crashing down amongst a bed of reeds. In the morning, as the sun lit up the new day, the fallen tree spoke to the reeds.

"How is it possible," Tamboti asked, "that I, who was so great and strong, find myself hurled down and broken? How it is possible that you, who are so light and weak, are still standing?"

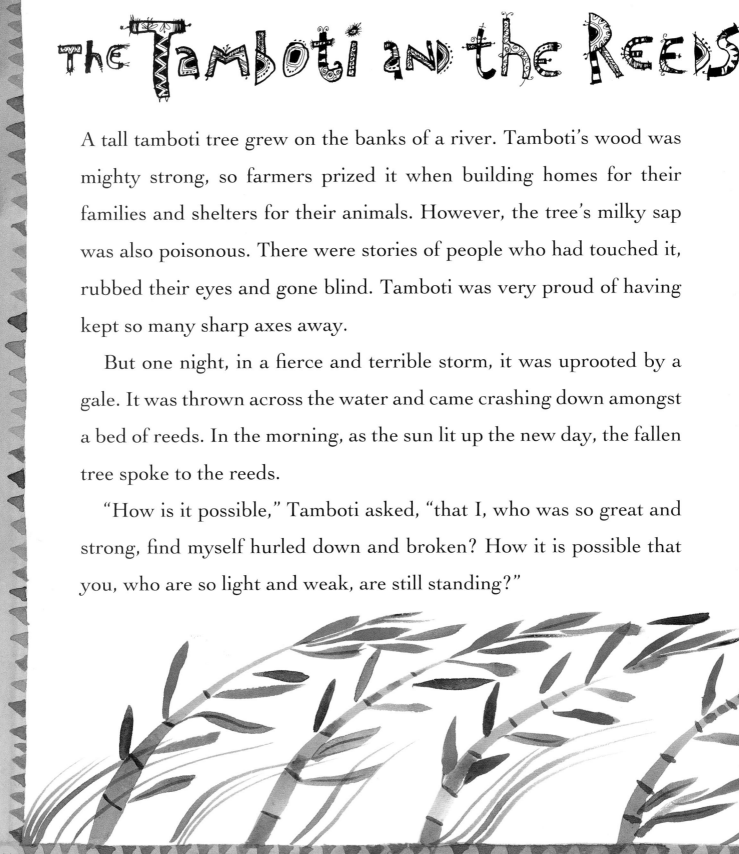

"Eh, you were too stubborn!" replied the reeds. "You tried to fight a storm that was more powerful than you. We know that we are weak. We bend and give way to every breeze. So a gale that will crush and destroy you, will simply pass over our heads."

~ It's better to be humble and bend
than to be proud and broken. ~

Tamboti – a tree with hard, dark, scented wood

The Grasshopper and the Ants

It was a clear blue day in the middle of winter and, for a change, it was quite warm. All summer the ants had stored away a heap of grain, but it had become damp and was in danger of going mouldy. So today they were carrying every piece of grain outside, to dry for a few hours in the sun.

A hungry grasshopper hid in the buffalo grass nearby, his orange eyes bulging out from his black and yellow head. Although he tried to stop his wings from twittering, his lime-green scales glinted in the sunlight. Even so, the ants were too busy to take notice.

The grasshopper watched them travel backwards and forwards until all their grain was spread out on the ground. Then he bounced towards them, nodding his striped black and orange horns to greet them.

"My friends," he sang out. "Can you spare a little food? I'm starving and I haven't eaten for days."

The ants clustered together in front of their grain. One of them stepped forward.

"What were you doing in the summer?" she asked. "Did you not store up food for the winter like we did?"

"Not me," said the grasshopper. "I was so busy singing that there was no time."

"Sjoe!" exclaimed the ant. "If you spent the summer singing, you had better spend the winter dancing."

All the ants burst out laughing and the hungry grasshopper was forced to hop away with an empty stomach.

~ It's best to think ahead. ~

Sjoe! – Really!

The Lion and the Mouse

A lion was asleep under a cabbage tree, in the shade of some rocks. In his dream he was about to sink his teeth into a big fat zebra when a mouse ran over his face and woke him. With a swoop of his paw, the lion trapped the little creature against a rock, ready to squeeze out its life.

"Oh forgive me, Morena!" the mouse squealed.

The lion liked to hear himself called "Lord" and waited to hear what the little thing would say next.

"If you spare my life, Morena," she begged, "I promise you that one day I shall repay your great kindness!"

"Ha, ha, ha, ha!" The lion burst out laughing. How could such a tiny little mouse ever help a mighty lion! But her voice was so serious that he was tickled by the idea. So he lifted his paw and let her scamper away.

Not long after that, a hunter caught the lion in a trap. The hunter had hoped to catch a zebra or impala or, if he was lucky, a fat kudu with swirling horns. Instead, tied up in his net was a furious, roaring lion. Swiftly the hunter ran off to bring friends who could help him drag the beast away.

But the little mouse had also heard the desperate roars. Realising that the lion was in trouble, she scurried to find him. As soon as she saw the great creature entangled with ropes, she set to work with her teeth. Gnawing here, gnawing there, she bit through the ropes until he was free.

"There you are, Morena," she declared. "You laughed at me when I promised to repay you. But now you can see that even a mouse may help a lion."

~ A little friend can also be a great friend. ~

Morena – Lord (Setswana)